The Eternal

Embers

Written by

Simone Kalra

"The Eternal Embers" published through Young Author Academy.

Young Author Academy

Dubai, United Arab Emirates

www.youngauthoracademy.com

ISBN: 9798398107814

Printed by Amazon Direct Publishing.

I dedicate this book to my
grandmother, for her belief in me
and for her love and support

Table of Contents

- Chapter One -

A Girl Called Maya

In a little, old house nestled in the woods, lived a spirited, young girl called Maya. Maya was ten years old and she cherished reading from a young age.

On many occasions, when she would start reading a book at night, she would exit the world of reading, become tired and drift away into dreamland.

Maya was so heavily influenced by all the spell books which she had read, that she constantly dreamed of being a fairy or a witch when she grew up.

However, people would laugh at her and tell her that she lived in a make-believe world and that her dreams would never come true. Maya didn't believe them. Nothing would stop her wonder and interest for magic.

Maya also loved to visit her garden, tucked away in the backyard of her house, and watch the flowers grow. She even had a small, special grotto in her garden for her to enjoy with all the creatures that would wander in.

Every day, she would go to school on the bus with her best friend, Kyra. Kyra lived in a cosy little house, right next to Maya's. She lived in a house similar to Maya's, with her three siblings and her wonderful parents.

Kyra was just like Maya, obsessed with reading books - and not surprisingly, the same ones. The two were inseparable! They were quite erudite for their age as they were always reading books like Harry Potter, and other books by well-known Authors; Enid Blyton and Roald Dahl, among others.

Maya and Kyra were as thick as thieves! Plus, they knew every detail about each other's lives. That was also how she got to know that Kyra was getting bullied by a boy at school. Seeing her friend having a tough time in school was like living hell for Maya. Maya would become very cross and gloomy whenever she saw the boy bullying Kyra.

Kyra would avoid the boy at all times, but when she was at school, she could not focus on her lessons, instead she would only keep thinking how she could ensure not to run into him in school. Helpless Maya wondered what she could possibly do to help her friend and prevent the boy from being mean. This would enrage Maya a lot as she felt helpless for Kyra. She wished she could do something about it, but her gut told her not to, as she was also afraid of the boy.

The best friends would meet up every day after school in Maya's grotto where they would enjoy cracking jokes and chatting about the spectacular creatures they would see; the lovely ladybugs, butterflies and frogs. It all just really blew their minds how beautiful the creatures were in their own little backyard garden.

One day, Maya noticed a very interesting golden butterfly gracefully flying towards the sunset. It was so special and captivating. Maya was literally hypnotised by it as its graceful wings carried itself through the air. But we can't blame her.

The charming butterfly had eccentric drop-dead gorgeous wings that were glimmering in the sunshine.

Sadly, Kyra snapped her out of her reverie and the butterfly soared through the skies far away from the human eye.

Later that evening, Maya was writing in her diary; an activity which was very personal to her and no one dared to even touch it.

Nobody was ever allowed to know what she wrote about. Her friends and family always wondered what she was writing about.

Dear Diary,

Today was a really fun day. As usual, Kyra and I were sitting in my grotto gazing at all the amazing things around us.

We saw frogs, butterflies, flowers, ladybugs and even more! Apart from that, Kyra kept cracking jokes that made me nearly fall off my seat!

She's my best friend in the whole world! No one can ever make me laugh so much!

Anyways, there's been something on my mind for a while now. Something really peculiar. It was so interesting that I was even hypnotised by it!

Let me get to the point. Kyra and I were wandering around when I saw···
A golden butterfly!

It was so beautiful and eccentric. I absolutely adored it! I tried to follow it, but Kyra tapped me on the shoulder and the butterfly flew away! I was so disappointed, but at least Kyra snapped me out of it.

Oh gosh, I'm so sleepy!

I'm going to head to bed now. Good night!
        Love,
            Maya.

As Maya was sleeping that night, there were some strange noises that seemed to be coming from outside. Carelessly, she ignored them.

Maya was in for a special surprise when she woke the next morning...

- Chapter Two -

Strange Noises

The next day, Maya kept hearing those strange noises all day; the same noises that were coming from outside her window when she slept the night before. It was kind of like a creaking noise... but why was Maya hearing these noises? What did they mean? Maya thought maybe they would end soon, but they didn't.

C-c-creak... Creak... CREAK!

That was it! She couldn't take it anymore. She started tapping and hitting her head, trying to get rid of the sound that was filling her mind.

Everyone in the class was looking at her.

"Oh Maya, what are you doing? You look ridiculous!" cried Kyra.

Thankfully, she stopped tapping her head. At least the teacher didn't notice what she was doing. Maya looked so odd. From hitting her head, she had faint red marks, she was okay though.

As she stopped whacking her head, the noises became unclear and eventually, they slowly dissipated. However, Maya had another problem; everyone started whispering about how bizarre she had acted.

Surprisingly, the teacher didn't budge. It was as if there was something in her ear. Oh gosh, Maya was so embarrassed. Kyra wasn't trying to insult Maya, but she was giggling a lot!

After a while, Maya didn't care. Everyone forgot about it. Let's just say it turned out to be a bad day for Maya.

Dear Diary,

Today was a really strange day! I kept hearing these weird noises in my brain. They went like··· creak! Creak, creak! Plus, they sounded like a broken door about to come off its hinges! I kept hitting my head in class and everyone was staring at me! The teacher didn't notice though.
But then when I stopped, everyone started whispering and I can bet that it was about me! Kyra kept giggling, but I know she means well!

(Angry but still ↓)

Love,
        Maya.

- Chapter Three -

A Book To Remember

Later that afternoon, when Maya was home after school, she was perusing through her books to find something to read. She wanted to find a different type of book from all the things she had read before.

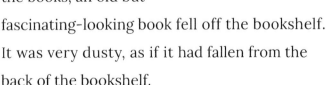

Suddenly, as she was thumbing through some of the books, an old but fascinating-looking book fell off the bookshelf. It was very dusty, as if it had fallen from the back of the bookshelf.

Maya instantly grabbed the book as she was curious about what it could be about.

It was a dark sage green book with a gold detailing on the cover. The book looked rather bulky and was quite large; having over a thousand pages. Maya thought this book was the best and possibly only discovery she had ever made.

She glanced through the pages quickly to find strange looking concoctions written down. They had peculiar-named ingredients like fluoroantimonic acid?

Maya had no clue what any of it meant. She wanted to find out but her mother called her for dinner. She kept her mouth zipped at the table as her parents would probably take the phenomenal object away from her if they knew that she had found it.

Maya made a promise to herself that she'd read more of this mysterious book the following day so she hid it under her bed for safe keeping.

For the entire next day, the only thing on Maya's mind was that rather quaint-looking book. What did it all mean? Why did it fall right in front of Maya? It was as if an unknown force in the book was beckoning her. Maya couldn't focus in class that day. Fortunately, for Maya, her teacher didn't care at all.

The moment Maya entered her room after arriving back from school, her eyes were fixated on the book.

An interesting stanza stood out...

Maledictio in hoc libro datura homini ad legendum. Maleficarum fasciculus carmine utetur ad pereundum centesimum librum lectorem. Hic liber admonet mundo 'Terram' quae veneficae veniunt.

By looking at the page, Maya thought that the phrases were just random words. She flicked through the pages until the 1000+ paged book was finished. Although, she was very disappointed. She thought the book would actually be interesting to read. To her surprise, it just looked interesting from the outside; upon skimming through it, it didn't appeal much to Maya. Most of the pages were filled up with random, odd looking pictures and stanzas.

Maya realised that she had absolutely no use with this book. She was extremely miffed with the useless thing just filled with writing and more writing, yet she did think that maybe she didn't quite understand it. It was just filled with writing, writing, writing and more writing. Like a petulant child, she threw the book in anger and stomped her foot on the floor.

Maya thought she needed some counselling from her diary...

Dear Diary,

Today was quite an unexpected but awful day, so far. For some reason, I found an ancient, dusty book laying around in my bookshelf. I decided to read it to see what lurked inside.

Guess what was inside that "amazing" and "fascinating" book?...

Random, puzzling words that looked like a 5 year old wrote it! Seriously! I mean, what's the point of making the book look interesting when it isn't interesting!

The book's pages looked like gibberish!
I'll never find anything to do with it!
Aw, I was so excited but then I found out
that there was absolutely nothing in that
book!
I don't even know what it was doing
there. Maybe I'll find out sooner or later.
Would you understand what it would say?

Probably not, because you're a notebook
I'm writing in and you don't have a
brain. No offence.

Love,
        Maya

When Maya was at Kyra's house the next day, the book suddenly took on a life of its own. It started rattling around her bedroom and suddenly started to shake. It hopped onto Maya's bed and started twirling. What was it doing?

Meanwhile, Maya was having a fun time over at Kyra's house. They were reading and laughing with a book in a little corner of Kyra's room. Sadly, the fun ended and it became dark outside. Maya had to go home.

She walked home and ate her dinner.

Then it was time...to read!

Maya ran up to her room just to find the annoying book again, laying on her bed, but not where she left it. This made her curious and suspicious so she decided to check it out again.

Excitedly, she went under her covers to get cosy. She slowly opened the book and abruptly, the book started flipping the pages on its own.

Maya was puzzled about what was happening...

- Chapter Four -

An Unexpected Trip

Maya was suddenly falling! She noticed a mesmerising spiral of wind come from inside the book that felt it would last for eternity, which made her feel like throwing up! The spiralling sucked her in and held her firmly with her room spinning around her.

She was thinking about what could happen next. Could she fall onto the other side of the world? Maybe she was in heaven? Just at the thought of being in heaven, Maya became very excited!

Perhaps she was going to be an angel!

If she was an
angel...

Well,
apparently not.

Maya was
flabbergasted at the hypnosis, but curious to
know about what was going to happen. This
experience was more bizarre than she had ever
experienced before.

The spiralling stopped, but Maya was very dizzy!
Round and round and round, and round! Maya
couldn't see straight because the spiral made her
see birds!

Once she was feeling better and not spinning
any longer, she felt puzzled at the sight of a
small girl, dressed like a witch. The girl was
looking at her in quite a strange manner. The

peculiar 'witch' held her hand out for Maya to stand up.

"Thanks," said Maya.

"You're very welcome!" replied the girl.

"My name is Beatrix, what is yours?" introduced the girl.

"I'm Maya, nice to meet you!" Maya exclaimed.

Beatrix then said, "Wait! You're Maya? You're the new girl, aren't you? Everyone has been waiting for you! The reason everyone knows is that the Enchantress suspected someone was entering the world of magical witchcraft. Welcome to the Moonlight Grotto! Here, live all the people that have been trapped inside that book! Before you say anything else, I just wanted to say that I'm so excited that you are here!"

Maya thought to herself that this girl talked a lot! But she was glad she had already made a new friend since arriving at this peculiar place. She honestly thought she was just dreaming.... Perhaps she was?

"I'm so excited that I am here as well, but I do have a few questions," replied Maya, "how have you all managed to live here for so long? Isn't it difficult?"

Beatrix answered, "Although I've lived here for 292 years, 3 months, 34 weeks and 23 days, it's so much fun to be with the people I love! Plus, here, we're immortal!"

"B-but what about your family? What about your friends? Didn't you just leave them behind?" Maya queried.

"I lived in an adoption centre but I always wondered who my true parents were. I didn't really have anyone to be with. But I'm here now! Plus, while you are here, time pauses, if you returned home, the time does not pass in the human world," Beatrix said in a happy tone.

Maya wondered how Beatrix had lived there for so long! Beatrix can't be lying though, as to Maya, she seemed like an honest girl and her story made sense. Maya thought that living in this fantastical world would possibly be better than living in an adoption centre.

The girls skipped along the fancy carpeted path, when Maya noticed the grotto surrounding her was quite interesting. There were lovely, ancient-looking artefacts everywhere. Although Maya got sucked into the book, which was quite a disturbing experience, she was excited to explore more of this strange world. It was after all, quite inviting and not at all scary. Maya was in the place she always dreamed of!

Beatrix was with Maya the whole day! They went around looking for something to fidget with. The two girls were jocular with each other, telling jokes and funny stories.

"What do you call a fish without an eye?" asked Beatrix.

"I don't know, what do you call it?" exclaimed Maya.

"A fsh!" chuckled Beatrix.

They skipped around the gigantic grotto, guffawing about all the things they were muttering about. Maya absolutely adored her new friend, but she felt guilty she might have 'abandoned' Kyra back in their world!

Maya suddenly realised that in her backpack, she had her diary! She had so much to write about and because Beatrix made Maya feel comfortable, Maya thought this would be the best time to write down her thoughts...

Dear Diary,
You won't believe what happened today…..I'M INSIDE A BOOK! You know that old useless book? Well…it sucked me in!
Who knew such a useless book could take me to a new dimension. Huh! Also, I made a new friend, her name is Beatrix! She's so sweet!

Beatrix has blonde, braided hair and she has a pleasant smile! She is- wait, I just realised something…

How am I supposed to get out?

Beatrix told me that she has lived here for over 200 years! If Beatrix has lived here for more than 2 centuries, then the reason should be that she couldn't get out!
Oh gosh, this is bad.

Really bad.

I'm going to ask Beatrix tomorrow.

Love,

Maya

- Chapter Five -

Peculiar Things

The next day, Maya and Beatrix were relaxing, having nothing to do, when Maya asked a question.

"Beatrix?" asked Maya.

"Yes?" replied Beatrix.

"If you have lived here for a very long time-" said Maya.

"292 years, 3 months, 34 weeks and 23 days to be exact!" interrupted Beatrix.

"Right... well if you have lived here for quite a long time, is it because you were unable to find a way out of this book?" enquired Maya.

Beatrix answered with a sigh, "Mmmm, I don't really talk much about it, but I will tell you!"

Maya leaned in closer.

"So 292 years, 3 months, 34 weeks and 23 days ago, I was just like you... except I was desperate to get out of this book. I went to go fulfil The Quest, but when I found out what it was, I rushed out of there and didn't complete the quest," Beatrix said.

Maya asked, "Well, what is this quest?"

Beatrix continued, "Oh it is so horrible! You have to visit this spooky cave where you meet this mysterious Emperor covered in lava! I don't know how he is alive, but like I said, he's a mysterious man, so, you have to basically walk through flames."

"WHAT?!" Maya howled.

"Yes, you have to walk through flames," Beatrix repeated.

"I-I-I can't walk through flames?! I'll burn to death! That Quest is impossible!" Maya rattled off.

"Not for people who have the power of Pyrokinesis...." Beatrix whispered.

"What's that?" Maya asked.

"Pyrokinesis is a power to manipulate flames! However, it's very hard to obtain and control but not impossible," Beatrix explained.

A girl like you had a similar power to Pyrokinesis before. She had telekinesis! Sadly, I don't think a lot of people have ever have had those powers before!" Beatrix explained.

"But how can we control if we have it or not? It isn't fair!" Maya complained.

"Well, you're actually right about that," Beatrix realised.

Maya thought to herself, 'Would she be trapped in this book forever?'

Hopefully not.

Maya decided to ignore the whole situation and enjoy her time in the magical world with Beatrix.

What could go wrong?

- Chapter Six -

The Quest

Maya decided that she wanted to explore the grotto further. There were lots of precious stones such as amethysts, emeralds, rubies, and many more types of crystals scattered everywhere! The world was filled with literal precious gems.

Maya soon realised that the grotto led to a larger cave. She thought she could traverse to find this spooky cave Beatrix had talked about, she felt like something was pulling her there.

She needed to find out more.

Maya really wanted to go and explore even further, but she thought that Beatrix would get in her way and stop her. Maya asked Beatrix if she could just wander around the massive grotto. She felt bad that she needed to lie to Beatrix, but she absolutely had to find out what force was pulling her there.

Maya started looking around, when she saw a sign that read,

DANGER!

THE EMPEROR RESTS UNTIL A QUEST IS NEEDED TO BE COMPLETED – NOT FOR ANY OTHER REASON.

She then remembered and thought to herself, 'Beatrix was talking about an Emperor who would be the creator of the quest.'

Oh, this was the spooky cave she was looking for! She slowly stepped into the rocky, dank sub -terrain and suddenly noticed a bright light coming from the distance.

Maya crouched down and sneakily strode through the cave until she reached a small wall near where the light was coming from.

She saw the sweltering flames dancing through the hallway. The flames were amber orange in colour and they threatened to engulf anyone who dared to go near. However, Maya didn't feel intimidated at all by the blaze in front of her; on the contrary, she felt an abnormal connection with the flames.

She decided then it was time. Maya thought to herself, 'you can do this, it'll all be worth it when you get home!'

She scaredly stood up and tip-toed towards the macabre man, wearing strange, but eccentric clothing, as well as a black and white mask, that had appeared suddenly.

"Hello," spoke the man in an ominous manner.

"I would like to complete the Quest, if I am worthy," Maya announced.

"Oh! Hmm, give me a moment," gasped the man.

"Maybe you can try, but I don't think you could possibly succeed," the man said.

Maya was willing to take the risk. Plus, she thought even if she got injured, it would only be in the book and not in real life, that is if she could ever leave.

Maya slowly stepped into the hallway of the scorching flames and ran along the side. She was cheating! However, she accidentally stepped into the flames!

"HELP! I'LL BURN! I'M TOO YOUNG TO DIE!" Maya cried.

But she realised that she wasn't getting affected at all by the flames! How was this possible? Did the Emperor put a spell on her? Were the flames fake and were just there to scare people?

Wait!

'D-did she have Pyrokinesis? That was impossible,' she thought.

Maya thought if she did, why didn't she discover it before she arrived in the mysterious world?

The Emperor looked amazed!

"Huh? No-one has ever completed the quest in over 200 years... How on earth did you do it?" asked the Emperor in a dark tone.

"I have absolutely no clue how I did it!" Maya exclaimed.

"Well, you did make it so now you can go home, I suppose," the man said.

Maya was delighted to be able to go home even despite having had a fabulous time in this newly discovered world. She happily skipped towards a big archway and over a lovely, leaf pathway that lead to a massive, hypnotising portal. She had never seen it before, perhaps it opened as she conquered the Quest.

As she arrived, Maya slowly stepped into the stunning portal and saw the exact same sight she saw when she was originally being sucked in!

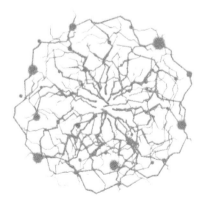

Whoosh, whoosh whoosh!

It still felt strange for Maya, going through the portal. It was a strange feeling. However, she slowly became used to it.

But then she suddenly remembered the way she ended things with Beatrix. She felt awful for her. She was having so much fun with her! Maya felt sick in the stomach that she didn't tell her that she went exploring further, and of course Beatrix knew nothing about her conquering the Quest and being able to leave the world where she met Beatrix.

At least Maya would be reunited with her best friend, Kyra. Maya then felt a little better as she was thinking about the fun she would have with Kyra and she realised that even though she had just had an intensely amazing, yet bizarre experience, she would be home and safe again.

Whoosh!

- Chapter Seven -

Back Home

Maya was home! She heard the sound of crickets chirping, owls hooting and leaves rustling on the ground.

She was in her own bed, and she had just woken up to a beautiful morning. Maya then remembered that Beatrix said that in the book, that no one ages!

So that means no time had passed! Thank goodness! Maya realised it was still Tuesday, but just that she got sucked in at night time, 'so then how was it now the morning?' she thought.

Oh no! She had to go to school!

Maya fumbled around with her alarm clock and realised that it was 4am. Phew! Maya decided just to relax a little and to laze around before she got dressed, ready for school.

She decided to read another book, but this time hoping she wouldn't enter a different world this time! Maya looked through the books, 'that one's boring, boring, boring, bo- ooh! 'The Good Sorceress,' she flipped through the pages and decided to read it.

Maya suddenly felt quite parched so she headed to the kitchen to get some water. She turned on the tap and poured herself a glass of water; cold, chilled water for her to enjoy, especially as overnight she had remembered the flames of the blistering grotto Quest!

She slowly drank some water to savour it, when she realised it was actually steaming hot! How? Maya poured it ice-cold but now, it was almost as hot as a fire!

She decided to pour some down the basin to then add in some cold water again. Maya poured cold water into the half-filled glass. Hopefully this would work.

Well, the answer was quite embarrassing...

'OH MY GOODNESS! IT'S SO HOT!' Maya screamed in her mind. If she had actually screamed, her parents would wake up for sure and get mad.

Maya felt as if her mouth was on fire! She started to insanely huff and puff. She slowly picked up the glass from the counter when the water in the glass slowly started to disappear.

She realised that gas was coming out of the water. Maya suddenly remembered a science experiment that she had done in school. She suddenly realised that when she touched the glass, the water evaporated! Was there a fire buried in her hand?

Poor Maya. She just wanted a drink of water! She moped as not only couldn't she drink water, she couldn't drink any liquid! and worse, any food!

Life without food wouldn't be life! Agh. Maybe she just had a fever? But there was no possible explanation for this. Why was this happening now? Maya woefully went back to her room to read.

Finally, some peace.

No hot water accidents, just Maya and her book. 'The good witch slowly pulled out her wand and-' "MAYA! WAKE UP! YOU NEED TO GO TO SCHOOL!" Oh no. It was 6:00am! She threw the book onto the shelf, quickly got under the covers and pretended to sleep. How cheeky!

Hopefully those drama classes after school would pay off.

"MAYA! Wake up! You're going to be late!" Maya's mum called.

"Do I have to go to school?" Maya groaned.

"Why else do I pay your fees for? Obviously, you will go! Not only that, but if you don't, you'll miss out on so much!" Maya's mum exclaimed.

"Oh fine!" Maya murmured.

She hopped out of bed and quickly changed into some decent clothes. Maya vigorously brushed her teeth and rushed to the dining table, ready for breakfast.

Maya saw some yummy pancakes on her plate!
Oh, it was pancake day!
She gobbled them all up
but wanted more!

'Mhm, so scrumptious!'

Maya checked to see if everything was in her school bag and then she skipped off to the bus, not daring to take a drink of water, or any other liquid for that matter until she figured out what was going on.

"Goodbye Maya!" Maya's mum gleefully shouted, as Maya plonked herself on the bus seat hoping that her day would be an uneventful and a quiet one.

Maya quickly put her hand on the seat next to her, saving it for Kyra. Maya was quite early on the bus, and she normally had to wait at this bus station for a while until students boarded the bus. She then decided to put her backpack on the seat instead of keeping her hand there.

Maya pulled out a book and quietly read it. After waiting for some time, more and more people arrived on the bus. But there was no sign of Kyra. The school bus was about to leave and Kyra was still not there. Maya hoped she would get there soon. One day of school without Kyra was almost like a nightmare for Maya!

Suddenly, the school bus engine roared as loud as a rocket launching; a sign that it was about to leave. Out of the blue, it was Kyra. She hurriedly entered and stepped up the bus steps and moved swiftly down the aisle of the bus.

Phew! Maya moved her bag off the seat and tapped her hand as a signal for Kyra to sit there. But, Kyra walked right past her as if Maya wasn't even there. Instead, she sat alone in the back.

"Why is she sitting at the back? She always sits with me!" Maya murmured in disappointment. "Is she mad at me or what? What did I do wrong!?" she said under her breath.

Suddenly, Maya felt very uncomfortable. She felt sweat dripping down her forehead and her hands were shaking.

She tried to ignore it but she couldn't. Sip, sip, sip. Maya drank some water. Although she couldn't drink water from a glass, she discovered that she could drink water from a metal water bottle.

It was as if she needed Kyra to live! Well, that was probably true.

Maya quietly read her book, thinking about Kyra for the whole journey. She thought maybe she would ask Kyra once they were in school.

Little did she know what would happen next...

- Chapter Eight -

A Horrendous Shock

After a long time of waiting, the school bus had picked everyone up and they had almost reached school. As usual, the bus passed the fro-yo shop, drove to the left by the flower shop...

Wait!

There was still more...

Straight past the local supermarket, slowing down near the bakery, which had quite mouth-watering pastries and more hand-made goods.

Delici- whoops, the bus drove away. Now crossing the humongous furniture shop and....there it was...

...Gardenia Elementary School.

The bus brakes suddenly screeched as loud as a jet engine! Its rusty doors opened as the bus conductor shooed everyone off the bus.

It was time for Maya to talk to Kyra. Their first lesson was Maths. Luckily for Maya, they were both in the same class. She was going to do it. Maya had the bravery to talk to Kyra. She had no choice as clearly there was something wrong.

She slowly approached Kyra, and before Kyra could say anything, Maya gave her a big hug.

"What happened? On the bus, you seemed really upset. Are you okay? Did I do something wrong?" Maya said.

Kyra stayed quiet and started to walk away.

"Kyra Grace Abbott, I am your best friend and you have to tell me what's going on!" Maya cried.

People started crowding around the two. It was

quite a dramatic scene.

"You shut me out! For three days, I called a hundred times, and there was no response from you! I was waiting at the grotto for hours! And I knocked on your door as well, and - did you guess? No response!" Kyra blurted out.

"Oh. I didn't realise that. I'm so sorry!" Maya said.

"Just sorry?" Kyra asked.

"Just please, I've never, ever missed a chance to meet you. I'm really, really, really sorry," Maya said.

"Maybe I can forgive you. But please don't do it again, okay?" Kyra replied.

They both sighed in relief, had a small hug, and headed to their first class.

Maya thought about how she missed the grotto meet-up. Hmm. Wait, she was in the book! That was it! But wait, Maya suddenly realised that time didn't stay still while she was in the grotto! How was that possible? Beatrix said that time wouldn't move forward in the book.... she couldn't have lied? Right?

In the middle of their maths class, there was a burning smell coming from outside.

"Huh, what could it be?" Kyra muttered.

Suddenly, the fire alarm started ringing; again and again and again- well, you get the point.

Kyra said under her breath, "Where is Maya? She's taking so long in the bathroom. She must hurry before it's too late!"

For Maya, she was just fine.

The sound of the faint fire alarm was unheard by her. She thought that everything and everyone was fine.

Except that they weren't.

All of the students were panicking, even the older

students who were supposed to be calming the younger ones down. The teachers were acting fine, but really, inside, they were traumatised. If they acted like they were inside, they would look as scared as a deer in the headlights.

Little did Maya know where the fire was.

In the girls bathroom, there was a peculiar smell. It smelt like f-

"FIRE!" Maya screamed, "THERE'S FIRE IN THE BATHROOM!"

Maya walked closer to the fire. Slowly, the fire became weaker and weaker as if Maya had caused it to die out. It truly did die out, but how could it be because of Maya?

She suddenly remembered, perhaps she would get in trouble for not coming out of the bathroom immediately after she heard the fire alarm!

Maya bolted out of the bathroom and made it just in time for the register check.

- Chapter Nine -

The Raging Fire

Approaching Kyra, Maya exclaimed, "Phew!"

"Oh my gosh. Where were you? I was so worried!" Kyra cried.

Maya replied, "The fire was in the girls bathroom! It wasn't that scary, it was actually quite strange. As I walked closer to the fire, it became weaker."

"That's weird, I've never heard of anything like that," Kyra added, "how is that possible?"

"THE FIRE IS GONE! I REPEAT, THE FIRE IS GONE," the Principal announced on the speakers, "ALL CLASSES BACK IN THE BUILDING IMMEDIATELY!"

"Maya, I think you saved the whole school from fire, with no intention," Kyra stated.

"I think I did," Maya said, "I'm a hero! A secret one though."

When lunch began and after the Fire Marshall's had investigated the fire in the bathroom, giving it the all-clear that everything was ok, Maya ran as fast as her sneakers could take her. and She locked herself in a bathroom cubicle.

She huddled in the corner, trying to match the puzzle pieces. The girl just needed some time to think. Numerous thoughts were flashing in her mind.

'Did she in fact have Pyr- no, that's insane.'

'Right?'

Maya took out her diary, and decided to write promptly.

Dear Diary,

Today there was a fire alarm at school. Not a drill. It was the real deal. I was in the bathroom when it happened. And guess where the fire was?

IN THE BATHROOM!

I saw it. I saw the dancing fire. Honestly, I wasn't scared. I felt as if I had a connection with it. As I walked closer to it, it became weaker and weaker. It was so strange!

So now, I'm here, in a bathroom stall, explaining everything that happened. Ah, I'm starving. I'm going to go eat lunch.

Love,

Maya

When Maya got home from school, she walked to the shrubbery in the garden and just wandered around.

All she needed was to clear her mind.

She skipped around in all the fetching flowers and noticed a bright red light flashing, coming her way. It kept changing colour.

Maya stopped to see what it was and then realised it was-

"FIRE!" Maya screamed.

The massive fire - which behaved like an inferno - went rushing towards her. Maya immediately ran away from it.

"Phew!" she exclaimed.

But she had forgotten something.

IT WAS STILL ON FIRE! Although she had narrowly escaped, the plants and the animals of

the grotto were in danger; she had to go back to seek help.

She started running towards the closest houses, and cried, "Someone, please help! The woodlands are on fire! We have to save the animals!"

But, the sight that Maya saw broke her heart. People were running away from the houses, and took all the belongings they could take with them, frightened that after the fire would engulf the shrubbery, their houses would be next.

Maya cried so much that her eyes hurt. Hearing all the animals' wailing, she was apoplectic with rage. Maya would have destroyed the fire if she knew how.

Suddenly, she felt a strange pain in her mind, it was a pique feeling.

Using all her torment, she was able to control the fire! So it was true...

Maya had Pyrokinesis!

How was this possible?

Apart from that, the question was, how did the fire appear? The village she lived in was so cold, you would have to wear five layers of sweaters in the winter! Forest fires would never happen in snowy weather conditions like the village's.

When Maya had bravely extinguished the fire with her powers, she noticed a small bonfire, with burned logs and ashes scattered around. So, the fire started from an unattended bonfire!

Maya suddenly remembered she had fire powers! She excitedly went over to the river and decided to try to test it. Maya thought, 'Come on water, heat up!'

She tried with all her might, but she couldn't.

- Chapter Ten -

Family Secrets

The following day, Maya and her mum were sitting at the dining table, reading the newspaper, when Maya's mum asked her, "Maya, did you hear about the woodlands incident yesterday? You were not home at the time, and I got so worried! What were you doing?"

She replied, "Uh..I..uhm I....was at Kyra's house! Yes... Kyra's house."

Maya's hands started heating up and turning red.

"You sure? And are you okay? Your hands are very red," Mum asked, looking worried.

Maya replied nervously, "Uhm..yes! One h-hundred percent!"

"Well, I actually called Kyra, and she said you were not with her, what's going on, Maya? Why are you lying to me?" Mum hollered.

Maya went blank and suddenly, tears rolled down her cheeks as she sobbed, "I'm sorry I lied to you, Mum. I was at the woodlands last night... I don't know what's happening to me. Somehow, I was able to control the fire. I didn't tell you because I didn't know how you would react. You must think I'm a freak, don't you."

Trying to calm her down, Mum replied, "Maya, it's alright. There's nothing wrong with you. I think it's time you knew. Our ancestry had a long line of people with supernatural abilities. You're not a freak, you're blessed."

"Really? That's so cool! But wait! You knew this day would come? How?" Maya asked.

Mum answered, "Your grandma's power was to tell the future. She said that a gift would be bestowed upon you, but we just never knew what the power would be or in what form it would take."

"So, if I go to her and ask her if the world would exist in the year 16890, she would tell me? And if I asked her if I would get good grades, she would answer?" Maya said, with wide eyes.

Her mum replied with, "Yes, she surely would!"

Maya's mouth was a capital O.

She couldn't believe anything she had just heard. But now it all made sense to her.

Getting to know that these powers were a part of her family's legacy, it soothed her and assured her that nothing was wrong with her.

But how could she control it?

She pushed her thoughts to the side.

After an eventful morning, Maya went about her day in a quiet, nonchalant way, trying not to think about what had transpired early in the day. She wanted to be a normal girl, with no crazy powers she couldn't control.

Maya went on acting like she didn't have these amazing powers.

Well, at least, she tried to.

At the end of the day, she went to her bus, sat down and pulled out a book. Maya thought she had succeeded in having quite a regular day.

None of the previous days were certainly normal for her. Finding out you have a secret power and using it to barely stop a forest fire that could've killed hundreds of animals, wasn't what Maya was expecting from the week so she was thrilled when the day didn't end with big news or her mom trying reverse psychology on her. Once Maya got home, she immediately rushed upstairs to write in her diary.

Dear Diary,
You won't believe anything I'm about to write···
I have···.PYROKINESIS!! (Fire powers)
Weird name, right?
Anyways, that's besides the point. Apparently all my ancestors had these crazy powers. Can you believe it?!

I just don't think I'm ready to tell Kyra yet. She's already going through so much, with being bullied. I sound like such a horrible best friend. But I'm scared too.

And I've never really seen how the bully treats her.
Is he mean? Is he just messing around? Or is it even more serious? I have no idea, but I'll try my best to take it off Kyra's mind.
        Love,
            Maya

- Chapter Eleven -

A Lesson Taught

The next day, Maya woke up determined to put all her worries and thoughts of the last few days aside, and to be her old self again.

She had thought about it the night before and had decided to keep her Pyrokinesis abilities hidden from everyone, hoping that this would help her return back to her normal life. But little did she know what the day ahead held for her.

Maya boarded the school bus, and grinned from ear to ear upon seeing Kyra. She plonked herself on the seat next to Kyra and soon they got to chatting. However, Maya sensed that there was something amiss about Kyra.

Normally, Kyra would make a few jokes every here and then, but the amount of 'jokes' she made during the bus ride was uncanny.

Poor Maya had to sit through thirty minutes of endless laughter and awkward banter. As Maya exited the bus, she couldn't help but think about how oddly Kyra was acting.

She kept making lame jokes and she kept laughing awkwardly. Her demeanour was unusual and out of character. It seemed that the bullying was getting way out of hand. Maya assumed that Kyra was trying to hide the truth from her. She had to do something about it.

Once they reached school, it was science class in the first period and they were setting up a lab experiment. They all had to pair up with a partner in preparation to study acids.

The partners had to do an experiment that was to involve chemicals and sulphuric acids. Even though it would be dangerous for them, they were trusted to be safe and listened closely in the lesson.

Not surprisingly, Kyra and Maya paired up. They were both keen to use those fascinating chemicals.

As the teacher was demonstrating the experiment to the kids, the bully that had always annoyed Kyra was whispering to his friends and not paying attention. Maya gritted her teeth and made an annoyed face.

His callousness irked Maya because she was expecting students to be serious as they were handling hazardous materials. But much to Maya's disdain, the boy continued with his buffoonery.

After the teacher's very long explanation, the children were finally granted permission to start the experiment.

Maya and Kyra put their gloves on and cautiously began to pour chemicals into a beaker, making sure nothing would spill on the table.

They were required to wait for about seven minutes until they were ready to add the final acid...Chloroform.

"Okay, now we need to add the c-chloroform!" Maya said, with a shock, "Heh, that's a funny name."

Kyra replied, "Maya, focus! We need to be very careful with this. Don't distract yourself."

"Right, let's get to work!" Maya said, with a sudden change of mood.

When Maya was slowly adding the final acid, the bully suddenly screamed, "HELP! THE ACIDS ARE CREATING A FIRE!"

When Maya and Kyra turned around, they saw

that some of the beakers had caught fire. The teacher told the students to stay calm and to leave the classroom. However, the students panicked and hurriedly left the classroom.

However, the bully was pushing Kyra, ensuring that she wouldn't be able to leave and would get stuck. But, a wooden plank from the ceiling fell, blocking the door for the boy.

In the ensuing commotion, the beakers that were on fire fell to the floor and soon, the fire had spread across half the classroom.

"I-I can't get out! Someone, please help!" the helpless, but cruel boy cried.

"You want help?" Maya said in an annoyed tone.

"Yes, please help me!" the bully said in a desperate manner.

"Really? I knew someone who needed help when they were going through a difficult time, do you know who that is?" Maya asked.

"N-no? Who, and quickly!" the bully said, sounding like he didn't care.

"Take a wild guess. My best friend, Kyra! I know you were bullying her, and it must stop!" Maya screamed.

"Uhm, I don't know what you're talking about," he lied.

"Stop lying, and be honest, or do you want to be stuck here?" Maya responded, in a very mad voice.

"Fine! But I was just messing around. Okay that was a lie, and I'm sorry. Just please get me out of here!" the bully cried.

"I'll help, as long as you never bully anyone else again, you hear me?" she told him.

"Yes, I'll apologise...now help me!" he said.

"Good, now you must not tell a soul about what I'm going to do," Maya said in a quiet tone.

Maya then used her powers of Pyrokinesis to stop the fire from burning down the school.

"How did you control the fire?!" the bully asked.

"Please just shut up. And by the way, I never want to see your face again, okay?" Maya said, feeling proud.

The bully replied, "I-I won't, I-I promise."

From that moment on, After that day, the bully never crossed paths with the girls, embarrassed by what he had done and also scared by Maya's final words to him. Kyra was also back to her old self again and Maya felt more relaxed and peaceful, now that she had accepted her power and who she was.

Life for the two best friends was back to normal.

The End.

ABOUT THE AUTHOR

Simone Kalra

Simone is a sprightly ten year old Dubai based author. She is an avid reader and writer and enjoys the works of Roald Dahl, Enid Blyton and Ken Nesbitt. In her spare time, she keeps herself busy with swimming, doodling, gymnastics and is often found cartwheeling and spider-walking around the house!

When she grows up, Simone wants to pursue her passion for literature and also dreams of becoming a veterinarian to make the world a better place for animals!

To follow Simone's publishing journey, please visit,

www.youngauthoracademy.com/simone-kalra

[Or please scan this

link with your device.]

Printed in Great Britain
by Amazon

23746464R00046